D1737258

1

BOYS WILL BE BOYS

By Rayne Havok

Copyright: March 2020

By: Rayne Havok

Cover design by: Rayne Havok

This is a work of fiction, if you find any similarities what- so- ever they are coincidental.

No part of this book may be copied or reproduced without prior authorization from the author.

Warning:

May offend

CHAPTER 1

Everett

"I *know* he did it." I'm trying to get Derek's attention by shoving his shoulder. "I know Ian put it in her ass, I saw the fucking video." That brings a roar of laughter amongst us all, echoing in the cavernous surroundings.

I get a punch in the side from Derek; simply returning the favor. It hurts, but the alcohol is soothing.

"See, I fucking told you, all girls are sluts. You just gotta tell them what they think they want to hear and their legs practically spread wider with each word," I say. "I've been telling you boys this since we were 14, bitches love the cock."

"Everett over here thinks he's gonna be writing some fucking tell-all story for everyone to read." Ian laughs. However, I just might. Girls are the weaker gender for a reason, they literally only think with their hearts, and if I've learned anything during all my years on earth, it's that, if you are controlled by something as weak as a heart- which is so easily broken- then you are susceptible to ruin. And ruin is my favorite.

"I knew he probably fucked her, but I didn't think she'd do it in the butt right away." Derek says, a little amazement coating his words. "She always talks about jesus and shit."

"That's exactly how I got her to say yes!" Ian's face lights up in excitement. "I told her I loved her, but we couldn't do anything that would lead to possible pregnancy, jesus would be so mad if we had to even think about an abortion, so we would safely do it another way." Ian's laughing at his own brilliance.

"Genius," Derek says, enviously.

I think so too; a little manipulation and you could have anything that you might ever want in life.

The topic of anything non-consensual came up last week in the halls of our high school. A girl in

Derek's English class had been turning him down for months without any real reason. All of our advice was getting him nowhere quick.

Her friend finally let Derek in on the little secret she was keeping, the one where she's gay and literally never going to give him the time of day.

I had told him to just take it from her. "A little rape never hurt anyone, so what, they cry about it to someone who doesn't really listen, then they become strippers or some shit." We all laughed.

"I'm down," Ian said, he shrugged his shoulders as if it were a normal conversation. "What's the harm in just taking the sex, just because a bitch is gay doesn't mean she can't enjoy some dick every now and then. Maybe she's gay *because* she's never had it good." After the laughter died down Ian picked up where his thoughts had let off. "We could even hide our identities with masks and whatnot. She'd be none the wiser."

I thought a little ahead. "Of course, then, we'd probably all need to get a piece of her. That way no one could rat anyone out for doing it." Not that we would, we could never do anything like that to each other.

I say, getting more riled up, "Girls are infuriating. The fact that men even need to communicate with them in order to get between their legs is sometimes not worth the effort. The shear bullshit we deal with in order to simply bust our nuts in them, like it's some fucking favor to men."

Derek jumped in, "I don't know when these women started thinking they were in control, its basically been since the dawn of time that women were put here, on this fucking earth, to please and fucking obey men." Derek puffed out his big chest, hyping us up even more. "Give me a time and a place and I'm fucking there, balls deep, or whatever."

"We should fucking hunt them and fuck them," I said. When neither of them stopped me I continued, I could feel the energy shift and I knew they would be in this with me.

After a few days of discussing such matters, English class girl was soon forgotten and the prospect of really and truly getting away with fucking a few strangers was evolving and taking us on a new path.

Careful planning, and a few days to perfect our idea, lead us to where we are now, the peak of South Mountain. Even though none of us are really hikers, we know the landscape and what to expect. Quiet, secluded, and far away from any prying eyes.

The shared binoculars, passing between us to keep a watch out for any game- that's what my dad calls the animals he hunts, so we've adopted it for our prey as well.

The night is creeping in and with that, it brings the cool night air. My arms goosebump and a shiver cools my veins.

We start making our way down the mountain. I toss our vodka bottle to the side, the remainder of the liquid splashing the rock it hit when the bottle shatters. Ian howls at the sky like a maniacal wolf and before I know it, we are all lost in the freedom of the night and the echoes of our ridiculous show.

"Shut up." I stop abruptly, putting my arms out to stop them from moving any more so I can hear what I think I just heard.

"Wha..." I put my hand over Ian's mouth to shut him up.

"There it is again. You guys hearing that?" I ask.

I see both of them strain to hear what only someone who knows what they're listening for can hear.

"It's laughter." I shift my eyes between theirs. Trying hard to get them to see what I mean.

"*Girls* laughter." I try harder, innuendo dripping from my words.

"Ooohhhh," Derek says, very much pretending to understand it. His brow furrows when he can not expound on his thought.

I take an exasperated breath and say again, "*Girls* are laughing. Sounds like they're having such a fun time out here all alone...on this mountain...far from anyone."

The two guys look at each other with big eyes and raised brows, finally having it dawn on them how they missed something so fucking obvious.

"I feel like the time and place might have just chosen us," I say. "The cosmic gods are looking out for us men tonight."

CHAPTER 2

Bri

I love these three girls to death, but I swear to god, one more word about how cute this boy is and how sweet this other one is, and I am going to throw myself over the edge of the cliff.

"Look how pretty it is with the sun falling behind the peaks." I try to move the topic to something else- *anything else*- for what feels like the hundredth time. Rose and Shay are still lost in their boy-crazed world. Lacy finally does look at the picturesque scene with me, after noticing that I've stopped to get a photo.

"You know them, babe, there is no disrespect to what you're doing for us right now."

I know she's right, the sisters have always been this way. Rose was born boy crazy and Shay followed suit to be close with her older sister.

I was hoping a little change in scenery would do some good for us, trying to see the things and do the stuff before we all go our separate ways. Even Lacy and I will be on our own journeys from here on out. In completely different states, it's breaking my heart again to think about. Only Shay will be here in a couple weeks. Being the youngest of the group, and tag-along for the most part, she still has some time before college takes her away. That is, if she chooses to go, she is *not* the sharpest anything in the box or shed.

Lacy tucks my hand in hers and squeezes her reassurances. The other girls are silent for the time being.

"Do you think coyotes fart?" Rose asks.

"Oh my gawd, leave it to Rose to say some stupid shit in a serious moment." I wipe my eyes before they can see I've been brought to tears. The other girls roar with laughter. I join in too when it hits me that this is so typically us, right here in this moment.

I pull Lacy with me and start our decent, long after we should have.

"Aww, I don't want to go."

"We have to go, Shay, its getting late. We don't want to run into a farting coyote, do we?" I coax.

The giggles turn to wild laughter after a beat and we are at it again, at least this time we are on the move. It feels as though night is falling faster than usual. None of us is particularly outdoorsy, and we are definitely *not* cracked up for being lost in the mountains, so I push forward a little faster.

It's silent except for the rustle of our feet, kicking the dirt in our abruptly hurried pace.

"There a reason we turned this hike into a fucking run?" Lacy teases me after catching up to my side. I didn't realize my breathing had increased so much, I don't even have enough to answer her. Somehow, an unknown fear had been nipping at my ankles.

I bend over, putting my hands on my knees and huff until my lungs have had their fill. "Sorry, I got the creeps." The other two finally catch up to us, I hadn't even known they were that far behind.

"We can walk the rest of the way, I guess." I joke, shaking off the strange unease the setting sun left me with.

We fall into a slower pace, unable to go much faster now that the darkness has taken over, brightness from the almost full moon lends quite a bit of light, but nothing compared to what was before the sun dropped.

"Howdy."

I stop abruptly, both seeing and hearing the stranger simultaneously. Rose steps on the heel of my shoe and crashes into my back, pushing me forward a step. A step I didn't want to take. One closer to this random guy in the middle of nowhere. I mean we are too, but still.

"Howdy." He says again, this time with a little wave. My guard is up and I'm instantly on edge.

"Hiii," Shay says, pushing passed me to get a better look at the stranger.

"I'm Everett." He's quiet a second as he looks to the side. I hear a faint shuffle of dirt. "This here is Ian." He says, just as a shape appears to us all. "The one back there is Derek."

We all turn to come face to face with a too-tall, thick, barrel chested tank of a man. Only he's wearing the face of a teenage boy.

"Oh, well hello to you." Rose says, completely un-phased by how strange this whole thing is. She juts out her hand for him to shake, "I'm Rose."

He looks down at her hand, back up to Everett, raises one of his eyebrows in amusement and slowly shakes her hand.

It's all the most subtle of gestures, but for some reason it's all happening in slow motion for me. My nerve endings are on fire. My legs are aching to get me the fuck out of here. Assuming I may have somehow picked-up on this very thing earlier when my feet new something I hadn't.

But, as I look around at the rest of my friends, they are smiling and seemingly ok with this. I want to chalk this up to unneeded worry, and I'm about to, but then I see the subtle shift in the boy on the side, Ian, he's approaching like a cat on the hunt. So slowly, that it's never realized until the pounce.

I feel an arm close tightly around my waist, "Hey, where you going?" I hear the soft whisper tickle my hair. I'm stunned, and my knees buckle, crumpling me to the ground. I'm further from my girls than I had been and it dawns on me that I had actually tried to leave.

Derek has his arm around the sisters and it looks like they don't understand what is actually happening right now. I don't necessarily either, but my instincts are fighting and wild.

Lacy comes to my aid quickly, sitting beside me, putting both her hands on either side of my face. I can see her mouth moving, but the rush of blood in my ears is overwhelming. She pulls my head to her chest and soothes my hair.

"Maybe low blood sugar or something." I hear the words echo from her chest before a strong hand pulls my arm up abruptly.

I see something register in Lacy's face, something akin to my own, something like understanding. She gets it now.

She takes my hand and I can feel her fingers tremble. Hers feel warm wrapped around mine, so cold from allocating the blood in my veins for use in more important parts of my body. Like my legs to get me the fuck out of here.

CHAPTER 3

Everett

Good thing Derek is so fucking strong because when this girl yells run, the other one makes a full fucking effort to get it done. She's pulling and fighting hard to get loose, same as this one. I have my fingernails digging hard into the flesh of her armpit as she struggles to gain traction on the dusty ground.

She manages to make a fairly big mess of herself, but not much else. I finally decide to pick her up by her middle, which does finally stop the dirt from being kicked up, but does nothing for my shins, which are the new target.

I start to whisper all her worst nightmares into her ear; she slowly gives up her fight until I finally feel her surrender entirely. "Good girl," I coo into her ear. "You know this could get worse, and you have no reason to believe that all of you could get away. You are bound to lose one, them's the odds. You play nice and everyone walks away. Maybe a little slower than before," I chuckle when her body stiffens. "But at least you'll be alive." I finish.

I'm able to finally take inventory of the situation after all the literal and figurative dust has settled.

The one I caught was on to us before she should have been. I'll have to keep my own eyes on this one.

Ian seems to have a good hold on the two he nabbed; tiny little things they are. I still don't think they understand fully what's going on. They look more confused than anything right now.

Derek is a little wet behind the ears, but he's strong as fuck, making the girl tucked neatly under his arm compliant. Although her face tells me she wants to rip me apart, she remains still, seething, but still.

"Alright," I say loudly enough for the whole group to hear me. "Tonight is going to go down as either the night you became a survivor or the night you lost yourself in the shameful misery of this." I chuckle at the confusion on the youngest girl's face.

"How old are you?" I lift my chin to her.

The girl in my arms answers for her. "She's 14, leave her the fuck alone."

"Oh, dollface, I'm asking cuz I ain't no pedo. Making sure her virgin cooch is all intact will be my honor." I pinch her cheeks between my fingers and make her lips pucker before licking the top one. She tries to pull away. "Damn, girl, I'm not trying to eat you. You just make sure you and your girls make us all happy and the baby can go with her virtue all wrapped up in them labia."

The look in her eyes would give any other man pause. But, I don't have that button, so I carry on despite the fire I feel on my face from the heat in her eyes.

"Like I was saying, we should all have a night to remember, for us, a night of bonding over broads, and a farewell to our youth, maybe. For you girls, a badge of survival. We will initiate you into the club of the 1 in 3. I think that's the ratio of you things getting fucked for fun." I shrug, not getting any truer statistics from anyone else.

Ian is the first to move. "Alright girls, just do what you're told, be good sports about this and it doesn't have to be violent." He pushes Shay forward, Rose tries to follow, but is abruptly yanked back. "You sit right here, on your knees," he tells Shay. "You move, even a little, and you're fucked...literally." I hear Ian chuckle. I'm glad we are all able to enjoy this together.

"Alright," I say, "we got a full moon and ain't nothing I like more than to see some titties glowing in the moonlight."

CHAPTER 4

Bri

Those words make what is happening a reality. This isn't a joke gone too far, this isn't some game, this is real fucking life, happening right now and I can do nothing about it. I'll lose the people I care most about in this world if I go off script. His eyes tell me how seriously he's taking this. The other two are only slightly less scary.

"Fine, you wanna see tits?" Lacy lifts her top up, flashing them to the guys but before she can pull her top back down Derek tells her to take it off instead. She flings the top unceremoniously over her head and onto the ground.

Like what you see?" she asks defiantly.

"I like 'em bigger, if honesty is what you're after," Ian says. I can feel Everett's laughter against my back.

I take mine off, feigning a bravery I don't really have.

"Those are more like it," Ian says pinching my nipple hard between his fingers before I can twist away.

"Let's go blondie, don't make us have to coax you into things, let's see those tits." Everett says, his voice growing agitated.

Her fingers shake, making it near impossible to get the task done. I can feel Everett make a move to go to her, possibly to hurt her, so I quickly move forward and lift her shirt over her head, reach behind her back and unclasp her bra to get this whole thing over with quickly.

"That was really hot," Derek says. The guys laugh and it makes me cringe.

With what strength I can muster, I say, "What now?" I can't think of anything I want more than to be done with this, and even though I'm rushing to get to the most awful part, my thinking is that, once we start, we can be closer to the end.

I see Everett's brows raise, impressed with my words. "Derek here is going first."

I see a flash of surprise from Derek; I can only assume they'd not talked about everything before they subsequently attacked.

"Which one you want, D?" Everett asks, tucking me under his arm, possibly to show I had already been taken from his selection. I try to mentally prepare for when my devil has his turn. My lungs barely contain the deep breath I need to take.

"I mean if you're really asking, I'd like dibs on blondie over there." Rose stiffens and squeals when Ian's grip tightens. Shay tucks her head in her hands.

"Nononono," She pleads as Ian talks her down into a sitting position.

"Ok, ladies we are going to need your help if you want this to go as seamless as possible," Everett says. "Girl, what's your name?" he says to me.

"Bri," I answer.

"Well, Bri, you seem to be the smartest around here, why don't you go help your friend get undressed the rest of the way?"

I glare at him.

"Please," he says, mockingly.

I go, but not a single cell in my body not fighting with me right now. I physically have to pull myself toward her while my body screams at me to run, to flee, to get the fuck out of here before my world is changed into a fucking nightmare that will have its claws in every second of the rest of my life.

"Babe, let me. Ok?" My voice shakes and I wipe frustrating tears away from my eyes so I can see her.

She sits back, not helping me, but doesn't stop me either, as I tug her jeans down her thighs and over her feet. I watch the cool night chill her body.

"Perfect." Everett takes hold of Lacy and shoves Derek toward a little to get him going. "You're up."

Derek turns pale and hesitates long enough for Ian to say, "Bro, let's go, she is not gonna fuck herself..." he laughs. "Unless, that's what you want?"

"I don't know..." Derek starts to turn toward Everett, who stops him midsentence.

"We are doing this. Here, is the place and now, is the time. Get your dick out." He leaves no room for further conversation in the finality of his tone.

Derek takes a breath and walks forward. It's surreal to see someone mentally preparing to rape someone. "I need her spread more, I don't want to get kicked." My stomach churns.

"Oh, for fuck sake," Everett rolls his eyes in frustration. "Girl," he yanks Shay up, practically flinging her at her sister, "Take her leg. You," he says to me, "take her other leg, make sure Derek doesn't get hurt. Keep her spread like she's having a baby."

I do as I'm told, for the sake of my friends. "It's ok, Shay," I sooth. Although nothing about this is ok.

I pull her leg open and look Derek dead in his eyes as he approaches Rose. But he doesn't look at me, he shares glances with the other two guys and the spot between her legs.

She fights and struggles more the closer he gets to her, but nothing prepares me for the sharp twist her body makes when he yanks his pants down and a big cock jumps out- the reality of our fates with it.

Everett jumps into action, puts her back in her place and hits her hard in the mouth. "I told you to play nice. Now. Play. Nice." Angry spittle hits her in the face.

She doesn't move anymore, not even when the blood from her nose runs down over her lips does she even flinch. She just closes her eyes to the nightmare.

Derek gets on his knees then tugs her body the rest of the way to him and pushes all the way into her without another word.

She cries hard, her body shaking in sobs but the boy continues, egged on by the other's cheers of encouragement.

I'm holding Rose's hand now, not her leg, Derek has taken that job over as he thrusts harder into her. His sudden aggressive grunts I can only assume are him finishing.

Rose scurries away when released, the raw skin on her back from the rocky ground now a bleeding rash down her spine.

I try to go to her but I'm tugged back hard into the arms of Everett who is whispering those same threats again. I glare at him, but he just laughs.

I stay back, watching Rose ball up and lie there in the fetal position, Shay next to her. I'm not sure if she is going to be able to calm Rose or if Rose is going to need to calm her. They're both a mess of sobs.

"Ian, you're up. You get that one." He points to Lacy, and in a flash, I see all the happy times we've shared together, all the times in my life she's been my rock and my best friend. The moments I needed her and she was there, standing strong and tall against anything in my way. I need to be that for her now.

I shake off Everett and go to her, wrapping her in my arms, I hug her so tightly I can feel her bones fight against me. "I'll be ok, Bri," and with that she is out of my reach.

I feel like I owe it to her to be a part of her horror so I watch. Ian takes her clothes off, it's so fucking foreign to me to watch a man undress a woman and if I didn't know what was actually happening I might think that this is consensual. Except for the sternness in her chin, I see no signs that she is in trouble.

Everett, beside me, runs his fingers across my chest. "We're up next." He pushes his crotch into the side of my leg and my spine stiffens.

I think about all the times I've heard people talk about their skin crawl and I thought I knew what they meant, but I was not prepared for the *real* feeling. It feels like all the pours along my skin collectively vomit.

CHAPTER 5

Bri

Ian is so much more aggressive than Derek was. And that's saying something when there is an oozing road-rash on Rose's back that will likely scar.

"Come here." I almost don't think Ian is talking to me, but when I don't respond quickly enough he actually stops what he's doing and swiftly pulls me along with him. He stands, completely naked, dick jutting out like some phallic monster. "Put your finger in her."

Everett whistles, "Oh yea, don't pretend like you haven't before, all those sleepovers weren't just full of pillow fights." He leans in close to watch, careful not to shadow the moon, which has been the only source of light.

"Just fucking do it, Bri." Lacy is barely holding herself together.

"See, she's fucking begging for it. I told you, bitches are all the same. Fucking cunts." Everett's anger is a full mask on his face.

I cannot watch myself do what they tell me, I gently slip my finger inside, but before I can pull it out Ian takes control of my arm and thrusts into her with me. I fight hard against him, but I'm not able to win and it seems the more I fight the more pain it's causing Lacy, so I just surrender myself and let him do it.

I can imagine how painful it is for Lacy to have my knuckles hit her this hard, practically punching her as he tries to force me deeper inside her.

"Stoooooop!" I don't realize I'm the one screaming until he does stop and all the noise around me ceases.

I stumble backward on to my ass and breathe heavily until I can come back to this world. All eyes on me, I catch the subtle movement behind them and before I can stop myself, I feel my eyes go toward it, regretting the second I learn the source.

I watch as Everett sees my distraction and looks behind the crowd in time to see the sisters getting to their feet and trying to make a getaway. And goddamn me, I am to blame for what happens next.

I hear the scream before I see what happens-- Rose being yanked back by her blonde ponytail, landing flat onto her back, instantly quiet after the air is huffed out of her lungs. The loud thud her head makes as it bounces on the solid ground shocking everyone silent.

Derek holds Shay under one of his big restraining arms. She is kicking for a release to get to her sister's aid when Everett shoves me aside to get to her.

"I see how I may have been too lenient, that's my fault, and this whole thing could have used a little more control. And I know what controls women-- pain. Pain will teach a woman quick." Everett indicates he wants Shay released; Derek does it while still maintaining a hand on her shoulder.

"Get on your knees, hands behind your back." He sweeps her leg and I can hear the crunch her knees make when they hit the ground. She squeaks and I understand why she can't follow the rest of her instructions in this state.

Her sister is lying eerily still on her back and Lacy sitting, arms wrapped around her naked body. A naked man inches from her face and the threat of her own pain happening right now.

Ian struts around her and grabs her wrists, tugging them upward hard. It forces her to bend forward and I shit you not, I watch a full conversation happen between Ian and Everett, and I know what they are going to do before it happens. I try to get up and help, I try to do something. Any-fucking-thing. But I'm not fast enough.

I am, however, in the path of Shay's blood as it splatters across my face after Everett brought his foot back and smashed it into her chin as if he's the kicker in a super bowl game. Her neck makes a crunch that I know will never be survivable. My heart rips open for her.

I can't breathe, I can't move, I'm hyperventilating, it's all too much. It's absolutely the most gruesome thing I have ever seen, until I watch as Ian releases her and crudely pushes her over with his foot. Her body topples over from the weight of her head, which lands horribly wrong in the dirt.

Shay, my sweet, beautiful Shay, so young and with so much left to do in this world, is slumped over, unrecognizable, her cute pixy-face a bloody mess rearranged and wrong.

Derek steps forward, putting his fingers to her throat. The fact that he can come that close to her and not flinch is mind-boggling.

"Ok..." Derek sounds angry. "This just turned into something else entirely. I never signed up for this."

"*We* never fucking signed up for this!" I hear Lacy shout, she's getting to her feet. There is blood smeared over her thighs. I look down at my hands and realize it also covers them. I feel the frantic need to flee again.

"You signed up for this exact thing, Derek," Everett says. "You notice how you can see my face? You can hear my voice? You can hear your name- your real fucking name, *Derek Farnsworth*, come out of my fucking mouth? Your real fucking DNA running down the thighs of the pretty dead girl over there? That's how you fucking signed up for this." He walks over to him, and in order to get there he steps over Shay's lifeless body. "You do the crime, although it is laughable to think using one of the come receptacles real quick could be such a thing, it is. You do the time, right? How would you ensure you not do the time?"

"I don't know, I don't fucking know. I just thought..."

Ian cuts Derek off mid-stutter and answers Everett's rhetorical question. "You get rid of the evidence," he says. "And these... are the evidence." He individually points to each of us. And as his finger reaches me, my heart falls to my feet. I should have fucking known.

CHAPTER 6

Bri

It's quiet for the briefest of moments. Long enough for me to realize Rose is still alive. Barely. Her throat is making a harsh wheeze and when I look at her, I can see the blood haloed around her head is quickly growing. She may be alive now, but she won't be much longer.

The only blessing she got was not seeing her sister's head watermelon wide open. The sound of that can never be forgotten.

I'm not the only one to notice her sound, all eyes are on poor Rose now. Ian bursts into laughter. "She sounds like fucking Darth Vader, I'm waiting for her to say she is my father."

"Don't mind him, girls, he won't be this insensitive when it's you lying there," Everett deadpans.

I try hard to catch Lacy's eyes, to get her attention somehow, without alerting the boys that I'm trying for that. I need to tell her to run, to fucking get out of here. So we can *both* go. But she hasn't even sat up yet.

Ian tugs his pants back up, but when he doesn't fasten them I feel the sick crawl inside me, rumbling inside my stomach, threatening its way up.

Derek has taken a few steps back, assessing the situation in front of him, after realizing the truth of what seems to been sprung on him as abruptly as it was on us. I'm thinking he may be our best bet out of this. If I could somehow use his remorse for a moment, I may be able to make him help us.

But as soon as my thoughts are headed in that direction, the words that leave his mouth hit me like a train and I know there is nothing more to do but fucking pray.

"Let's finish these ones up then."

"Good thinking, D." Everett claps him on the shoulder and wraps his arm around, tugging him in my direction. "And it looks like I'm up."

I scurry as fast as I can, knees scraping against the sharp rocks away from the look in his eyes. I make it to Lacy, pulling her arm hard to help her off the ground. Pain from an unknown source erupts in my head and turns into a ringing so loud, it's deafening.

"Your turn, Bri," Everett coos close to my ear, his body pressed tightly against mine.

He tells the other two to make sure Lacy is a "good girl" while he gets his turn, as he struggles with my shorts. I do nothing to help him; I remain dead weight until he pushes me onto my stomach, flat against the ground, making it too easy to get me naked.

I feel him against me, hard and breathless, grunting loudly from his exertion.

The fire inside my virgin hole as he enters me manifests in my throat as a siren scream. He doesn't even seem to notice he's the first man inside me, and more than likely my last, if this devil has his way.

I can feel his anger raging hotly inside me, all his hatred, for not only me, but also the rage that has somehow built inside this young man over time. This isn't sex for him, this isn't for his pleasure in the normal sense. This is for his release of all this pent up aggression.

I was hoping it couldn't get worse, but when he wraps his hand around my throat, pulling so hard my neck feels as though it will fold or break, I realize he's just getting started. I'm out of air quickly and the pulse in my ears is pounding, throbbing down my spine. Then he loosens up to let me breathe, but only long enough to feed my lungs a small portion of what they crave before he does it again.

Over and over until I'm nauseated by the rush of blood fighting inside my head. I throw up. My stomach heaves and as he lets go of my throat the next time the vomit rushes out of my mouth.

Laughing, he shoves my face into the wet dirt and rubs my nose into it. It smells sour, like fear, and makes me want to throw up again but there's nothing else.

He slows down and finally stops, tiny stars flood my field of vision. Realizing he's just come inside me, disgust boils deep within my chest. If I could think any less of him I would, but he's the scum of the earth-- the *waste* from the scum of the earth.

A monster masked inside a normal looking teenage boy. Society's shame.

I think he will get off of me and that I'll have time to formulate our escape as he unwinds but I don't get the chance.

He flips me over, looking me right in the eyes and shows me the folding pocketknife; he shoves the sharp edge against my cheek and slices hard. Pain erupts as the hot liquid rips from my skin.

The knife is then jabbed into my side and pulled out. My stupid ass thinks only of my 5th grade teacher saying that you should never remove an object that has been stabbed into you. That you might die from blood loss and that it's better for the medical professionals to do it.

The second stab reminds me that his goal is to kill me, not hurt me. But I'm not able to fight him. I just lie here, letting him do this. The shock to my body is so overwhelming I'm not able to pinpoint a way to help myself, I'm barely able to focus my efforts on breathing, something so natural when you're not in the throes of your own murder.

I reach my hand in the general direction of Lacy, but I don't make contact. I am able to turn my head and see that the other two boys must have already had a turn with this knife. Blood covers her entirely and they are practically glowing in it from the moon light on their naked bodies.

I look back up at Everett who has set the knife aside, and foolishly, I'm about to be grateful but then I feel him spread my legs again. His hand feels hot against my skin, which seems drastically colder than a moment ago.

His nightmarish grin unnerves me as he shoves his fist inside, deeper than he should, the pressure is almost more than I can take. He's rough about it and I can feel the bile building as he stretches the inside of me.

I try to say some badass thing that would make women around the world hoot and also so profound that he changes his ways, but I don't think my garbled, wet coughs are being understood that way.

I no longer feel him, or me, for that matter. It's hard to keep alert and I realize that if I no longer fight, I can just go and it would all be over. The thought is warm and very welcoming. I let myself succumb to that warmth, and then the dark follows.

CHAPTER 7

Bri

The first thing I can feel is a subtle ticking in my neck, I focus on that, letting it become stronger and more rhythmic.

Then my lungs open up and I'm able to take small breaths. If I go too deep though, my chest aches and the pain returns.

I try to open my eyes but there is only darkness, a musty, dirty, dank darkness.

Shifting my body is impossible, there is a weight on me I'm sure I would rather not analyze, but now that I know I survived, I must do this.

My fingers feel around, but every movement has the dirt sifting and rearranging.

I'm afraid, I don't know if I should alert them- if they are still around- to the fact that I'm alive. But, I must do something, my lungs are screaming at me for a full breath, one absent of the mush.

I wave my arms, building a momentum strong enough to move the dirt, kicking my legs when I can feel it give, the pain in them threatening to worsen if I do the wrong thing. But my mind is fascinated at the thought of escape, so I push it down and try to persevere.

I feel the cool air and fight harder to free myself. The first exhilarating breath I take is cold and burns my lungs, causing a deep cough to erupt. I take my time and reacquaint myself with the task, pushing the rest of my shallow grave away from me. It's morning now, I crane my neck to see the suns placement and realize- a fairly late morning.

I look at my hands, filth and blood covers them, and I absently try to pick the grit from my fingernails. I'm still naked, bloody mud covered, but naked.

My strength has returned and I know I must try to make it down the mountain, find some help, and pray to fuck I can get someone to listen to me.

I survey the area when I'm able to stand and realize my friends are under my feet, I can't tell where, the gravel is loose all around, but I know they're there. I step carefully, not really wanting to face that truth head-on just yet.

My core is sore, my insides bruised, and it makes hiking near impossible. The bleeding has stopped, luckily- the mud possibly acting as a clotting agent.

I stumble multiple times, never actually falling, finally making it all the way to the bottom just as the sun slides in above my head.

The car is still here, same as yesterday; when it was the only one in the small parking area. I get the magnet key stuck under the wheel well. The thought of my father brings tears to my eyes; all his over- protective tendencies feel so refreshing to me right now.

I'm barely able to get behind the wheel from the shaking cries. I cough, choking on a sob, spit the mud from my lungs and mouth onto the ground and start the car. A new determination grows inside me to see this whole thing through.

I wonder what the best course would be for me, I need a doctor, possibly surgery, but I know that if I go to the hospital, they'll likely start in on that process right away, possibly contaminating evidence in the process. And I can't risk that, I need the police.

The station is only a couple miles away and I'm able to make it there quickly. I pull down the visor and foolishly look at myself, mostly out of habit to check my appearance before going in anywhere. But I'm taken aback by how shocking I look.

Aside from the cut on my cheek, I had imagined some dirt and crud, but my entire face is misshapen and swollen. My eyes are red, veins swarm the whites, and my left eye is swimming in blood. My nose is crooked, and caked in blood. The slice across my cheek is actually gaping. I watch the tears leak out and fall from my chin. I wipe them away angrily and slam the visor up and out of my way.

Leaving the car with as much gusto as I can muster, heading for the glass windowed entrance I pull the door open.

A woman in uniform practically falls on her way to collect me just as relief crumples me to the floor, lightheaded and dizzy from the relief.

"Get your asses in here!" she screams, her hands fussing all over my body. "God damn it, get the fuck in here!" Her panic is worrying me. My heart takes off and feels like it's trying to break out of my chest.

"I'm ok." I try to reassure her, and hopefully myself. I hope I haven't made the wrong decision by coming here.

"You are *going* to be ok, honey, but right now, you are *not* ok."

I wake up to the woman smoothing my hair; there are three men in police uniforms around me. All waiting for me to come to, I suppose.

When I try to sit up, she gently helps me. My muscles feel like rubber and I'm sore all the way to my bones.

I have to clear my throat before I can speak, she hands me a cool glass of water that dribbles down my chin, my swollen lips unable to accommodate the eagerness of my thirst.

"I need help."

"Oh, honey, we can all see that much," she says, a little drawl to her voice that is not native to this side of the country.

"We were attacked, my friends and I. They're not alive anymore," my voice hitches, but I try to make it through. "They're buried on the mountain. So was I, but I got out."

Her hand flies to her throat and she gasps, "You don't mean you were buried?" her eyes pleading with me to confirm her doubt.

I nod. "Three boys, teenagers, maybe my age, I'm 18." I'm rambling, I try my best to make myself more understandable. I start over, "Three boys attacked my friends and me last night while we were hiking. The four of us were heading down when the boys found us. They just sort of appeared, it gave me the creeps instantly. But we weren't able to get away. They raped my friends. Me too. They raped me too. I watched them kill my friends and then I woke up under ground."

The tears flow freely now. She hands me a tissue.

"Gabe, why don't you see if you can find a map so she can point us in the right direction?"

She turns back to me when we are alone, "Do you think you'd be able to do that? You know the area well enough to get him there?"

"I can try, I mean, I know where we were." I am handed a map, the zigzagging lines are all a blur to me, I don't know if I could do this under normal circumstances, and I'm at a complete loss for where to begin.

"K, this area is the marked hiking trail, is this where you guys were?" he looks at me, encouraging me with his eyes.

"Yea, we were definitely on the trail, that's not where I woke up though. The trail dirt would have been too solid to dig there. My friends are somewhere in the brush area off the trail, maybe the last third of the way down." I shake my head, knowing I won't be much help in precisely finding a way to help them. "I can show you." I'm on my feet quickly. Knowing this is far more important than my pain, I'm able to pull myself together after a few deep breaths.

"I'll grab the keys, Gabe, you get her somethin' to wear."

That leaves me alone in the room for only a second before she comes rushing back in.

Gabe hands over an arm full of clothing and turns his back to me for privacy. The woman, whose nametag says Gwen helps me dress, pulling away the sheet someone had covered me with. It hurts to do the simple movements needed for such a simple thing, but I don't let on how bad it is. Unless she's looking at my face cringing she might not be able to tell.

I don't dare look down at my body, I keep my head trained on the stark wall across the room,

I can't see myself like this. It will be too much for me, and right now, I have to get them to my friends, we have to go get the evidence.

We head to the car, Gwen helping me walk and Gabe opening the doors and waiting for us patiently. He gets behind the wheel and Gwen is in the back seat with me. It feels nice to have her here.

"You want to call your parents, hon?"

I hadn't actually decided what to say to my parents yet, I don't want them to come in all frantic and miss the important things, which are my friends. I just shake my head. "I'll call when I know my friends are found." I give her a half smile and feel my lip rip open. I quickly turn away from her to wipe the blood away before she can see.

We park where I tell them the girls and I had yesterday and point him in the direction of where to find them. With me unable to really hike right now unless I have to, I'm left in the car with Gwen, hoping I gave Gabe enough information to find them.

"When we get you back to the station, I'm gonna have you call your mama," I can see the sadness in her face.

"You have kids?" I ask, because it looks like she's trying to navigate what it would feel like to have this news brought to her door.

She nods, "I'd do anything for them, including rip apart someone who'd hurt 'em." She takes a determined breath. "We are gonna do everything we can to get these boys who did this to you. Get you a meetin' with the sketch artist and get you a line up, all the things. You saw them right? Would you be able to describe 'em?"

"Yes, I can do even better, I know their names."

She frantically searches her pockets for a little notebook she pulls out. "Why didn't you say you knew the boys?" she struggles with the pen cap, her hands shaking a little.

"I don't know them, they introduced themselves to us...before, you know."

Her face is full of shock, like me, confused that they had done that.

"Ok, I'm ready." She's pulled herself together and is poised with her pen at the ready.

"The first one, his name is Everett, blonde kid, tall and lanky, but strong." Her pen moves quickly, scribbling the info on the paper.

"Ian was the next one, kind of a jock, dark hair, curls hung in his face. The third was Derek, he was a giant, thick and muscles, more so following the other boys lead, I was hoping he'd be helpful to us, but he turned out just as ba..." my sentence fades when I realize her pen has stopped.

She fumbles for the door, "Gabe's back, you hold tight honey."

CHAPTER 8

Gabe

"I found where the girls are, there's not a trace of them unless you knew where to look. These bastards are in for a real rude fucking awakening," I say to Gwen as she nears me. Her face full of panic and for a second I think the girl in the back of the cruiser is in trouble. Damn it, I knew it was too risky to bring her here before the hospital.

"Gabe, she knows who the boys were."

"That's great! Are they in the system, are they known to us?"

She nods and I'm confused about her lack of excitement. "They're known to us, *specifically*, its Everett and Derek." She steps back from me, like I'd attack her for the information.

"*My* Everett and *your* Derek?" I ask, my heart thundering in my chest. I take a deep breath, shaking my hands out to alleviate the tension. "Was this confirmed by physical description? You know all teenage boys have the same look about themselves at this age. How did you pull this outta what she said?" I ask her, hoping for a chance she's wrong. Gwen is a good officer though, and it's not likely she's telling me this on a hunch. But still.

"She had their names, full description. Ian was there too. Dane is not gonna be happy to hear this either." she says mournfully.

I go off, "No one's going to be willing to hear this shit! A bunch of cop's kids killing- brutally killing- and raping these girls! The town is gonna have our badges and the kids' heads. This is real fucking life and those boys aren't gonna see the outside of a prison cell and they're barely fucking adults." I'm thinking wildly about all the things these boys have just gotten themselves into.

"I can't have Derek in prison." Gwen says, meekly.

"I know that. You think I don't fucking know that? The boys will have the book thrown at them, this is it for them, their whole fucking lives are over. We won't be able to explain this away with some 'boys will be boys' shit." I see the panic rising in her face, but I can't stop myself, the

consequences are insurmountable.

CHAPTER 9

Gabe

Tears are flowing quickly down her cheeks; my words are too much for her. "I'm sorry Gwen, that was too far, I'm sorry." I try to comfort her, but there is no way to ease this burden.

"Derek's future is too bright. He won't be able to handle this, it will be too much for him." She grabs hold of my shirtfront, gasping, as something just dawns on her; looking up at me, all color draining from her face. "You know what they do to young boys in prison. You know what they do to rapists in prison!" She's frantic now.

And I also know what they do to boys like *ours* in prison. "Cops' kids, no less."

I catch her before she crumples to her knees. "Oh my god, we have to *do* somethin'." She shrieks.

"The something you are referring to is…?" I ask, leaving it open at the end to see where her head is actually at.

"She knows them. Her testimony will hol' up, she took us right to her friends. And for fuck sake, look at 'er! If her friends look even *half* as bad as she does, they'll be done for. And god forbid one of them not be 18 yet, that's killin' a kid, the jury will end their lives, they'll get the needle for sure. She'll kill our babies if we let her do this."

CHAPTER 10

Bri

They get back to the car. I turn around in my seat, pretending I hadn't been watching them, the thick glass left me wishing I could read lips. The door comes open and I'm expecting Gwen to reenter the car, but it's Gabe reaching his hand inside for me to take.

"Come on, we need your help."

I grab his hand and let him help me out, Gwen is holding back, not looking at me. It feels strange, but this whole situation is strange, so I don't let it get to me. I look at Gabe, who is talking now, confirming what I had told Gwen about the boys. Yes, I know their names, yes, perfect description. And, absolutely, I can recount everything they did to us. Even have DNA.

I expect him to look happy, case closed and all that shit. But he's not, I can tell.

"What's wrong?" I ask hesitantly.

"Nothin's wrong, honey," Gwen comes quickly to me, putting an arm around my shoulder. She turns me around and starts to walk up the mountain.

"Did he not find the bodies?" I ask, wondering if that's the reason for the unease.

"No, he found them, right where you said they would be."

"Then what are we doing? I don't want to see them. If you're trying to make me identify them or something. I would really rather do that later. I need to call my mom. Just let me do that now." I'm starting to panic as her grip is tightening against my struggle. "Please just let me go."

The air is squeezed out of my lungs when Gabe comes behind me and hoists me into the air, strong arms gripping my torso. I feel the wound at my side tear open, the blood flows quickly down my leg but I still manage to kick and fight. "Why are you doing this, you're hurting me, please!" I can't imagine what the reason for this could be, my mind is reeling.

I fight harder when the spot I dug myself out of appears. I can't see my friends right now. I can't be here. I shouldn't have to do this. I should be at home getting ready to start college and be excited for everything I could do with my life. I should not be here where my friends died. *Where I fucking died.* I'm crying now and I can't stop. I don't have it in me anymore, I'm so tired already.

Gabe sets me on the ground and before I can run, which a huge part of me screams to do, but Gwen is here, arms on her knees to bring her face to my height and her eyes are full of tears, momentarily confusing me into submission. "Honey, I'm sorry those boys did this. I can't imagine the horror you and your friends went through last night. I can't even fathom what it must have been like to go through that. You girls had a real horrible night." She wipes the tears off my cheeks gently. "And it pains me, it really does. I can think of a lot of ways those boys would have the same fate dealt to them, over and over. They would be raped and hurt and stabbed, for more than *one* night."

I nod my head vigorously. "Exactly, karma will take care of this." I'm eager for her to understand that I know all of this. "I know."

"I just don't have it in my heart to let my boy go through that," Gwen says.

I don't understand what she means right away but I ask, "Which one is yours?" when it dawns on me.

"Derek, he's my only boy, the sweetest thing really. I know you saw a little of that last night, you told me remember? Everett is Gabe's kid, his only one."

"Great parenting," I say sarcastically. "What now? You want me to keep quiet? Say I don't know who did this to me? What?"

"I just want you to take a step back," Gabe says.

I look behind me and see that that would mean for me to get back into the hole that I had dug myself out of just hours ago.

"You're going to kill me? Just like your kids did. And you fucking wonder what's wrong with this world!" I shout, exasperatedly.

I don't take that step back, I stand my ground, disgust plastered on my face. I open my arms wide and close my eyes, drawing one last breath to say, "you better pray the devil doesn't let me out of my cage," before I feel the pain slam into my chest. Quickly, air rushes from my lungs.

It's agonizing not being able to draw in a breath, but that ends when the next shot I feel hits me in my head.

CHAPTER 11

Everett

"Get your ass in here boy." My dad says to me, not uncommon when he's had a shitty day at work. I, on the other hand, cannot be brought down from the night we had. Not a single thing could ruin that.

"What?" I ask when I see him in the kitchen. I realize he's home earlier than usual when I notice the clock on the stove.

"You know, I do a lot for you, most of which you don't even understand at your age," he says.

I sit on the stool at the breakfast bar, feeling this is going to be one of those long father son talking to's. "I know you do dad." I hope that it speeds this process up if I'm saying all the right things.

He comes to me, stopping only when his foot kicks the chair leg. He puts his face directly to mine, our foreheads touching. "There's only one time I clean up a mess like this for you." Before I can ask what mess he's talking about, he tosses my baseball cap at me. The same one I left on the mountain last night, not realizing it until after I arrived home.

"Where did you find this?" I manage to ask innocently before the back of his hand makes a connection to my jaw.

"One fucking time, Everett. You make a decision like you made last night, and I won't get rid of your evidence again."

"What…"

He quickly cuts me off, "a girl came into the station today, messed up worse than you could ever imagine. Well, I'm sure *you* could imagine, since you were the one who did it."

He sees me realize what this is all about. "Dad, I…"

"Next ones on you, boy." He walks out of the kitchen.

We just have to be more careful about the evidence next hunt.

The end.

More by Rayne

Degenerate

The Boy

The Embalmer

XXX

My Christmas Story

Devour

Retaliation

app

Made in United States
Orlando, FL
15 August 2023

36082648R00061